IN THE GARDEN OF
BADTHINGS

POEMS BY
DOUG MACLEOD
PICTURES BY
PETER THOMSON

PUFFIN BOOKS

To our parents

In the Garden of Badthings

Vampires dance beneath the moon,
Eating blood plums with a spoon,
Killerbeasts and unicorns
Nestle down amongst the thorns,
While, at the top of every tree
A dozen vultures smile at me.
'Welcome home!' the vultures say,
'We're sorry that you ran away,
But, now you're back in our domain,
We're sure you'll never leave again!'

Car Attack

On last year's Halloween
A car hit Auntie Jean.
Unhinged by this attack,
My Auntie hit it back.

She hit it with her handbag
And knocked it with her knee.
She socked it with a sandbag
And thumped it with a tree.

On last year's Halloween
A car hit Auntie Jean.
And now, my Auntie's better
But the car is with the wrecker.

Brian

Brian is a baddie,
As nasty as they come.
He terrifies his daddy
And mortifies his mum.

One morning in December
They took him to the zoo,
But Brian lost his temper
And kicked a kangaroo.

And then he fought a lion
Escaping from its pit.
It tried to swallow Brian
Till Brian swallowed it!

Yes, Brian is a devil,
A horrid little curse —
Unlike his brother Neville
Who's infinitely worse!

Screaming

I hate the sound of screaming —
When horrors pull your hair,
When shutters bang and doorbells clang
But nobody is there.

When yellow eyes are gleaming,
But they are all you see,
I hate the sound of screaming —
Especially when it's me!

Brenda Baker

Brenda Baker, quite ill-bred,
Used to cuddle fish in bed.
Tuna, trout and conger-eels,
Salmon, sole and sometimes seals.
Barracuda, bream and bass,
She cuddled them, until — alas!
One unforgotten Friday night
She slept with two piranhas,
And, being rather impolite,
They ate her best pyjamas!

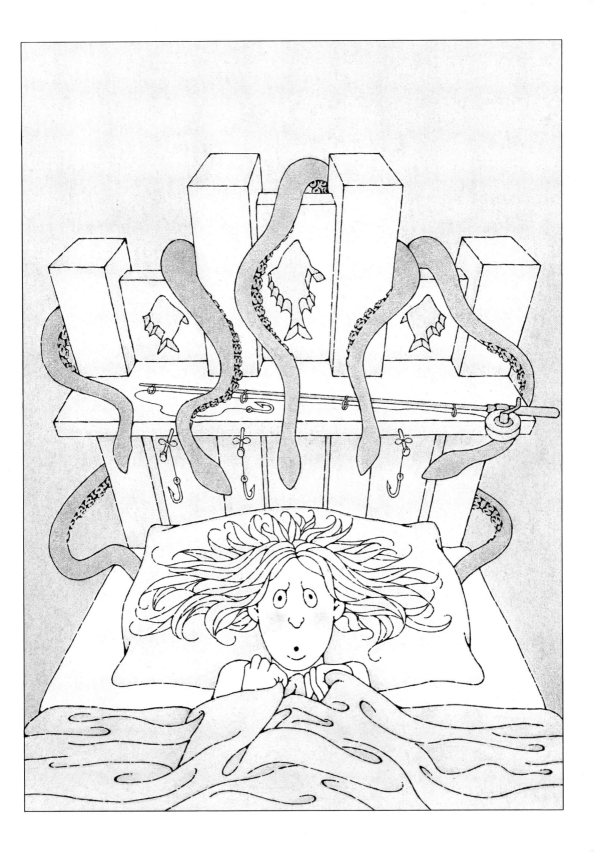

The Human Fly from Bendigo

My favourite uncle, Tim McFife,
Was very keen on circus life.
He had an act which stole the show–
'The Human Fly from Bendigo'.

Each night, he showed his expertise
And balanced on the high trapeze
Then, spreading both his silver wings,
He fluttered round the Roman rings.

As spotlights blazed on Uncle Tim,
A thousand eyes were fixed on him,
A phantom flyïng to and fro –
'The Human Fly from Bendigo'.

And so he stunned them every night,
Dressed up in foil and party lights,
Suspended by a handy wire
To keep him flying ever higher.

One dreadful night, the wire went slack
And Uncle landed on his back
But, ever faithful to his pride,
He kicked his legs, buzzed once, then died.

Lovely Mosquito

Lovely mosquito, attacking my arm
As quiet and still as a statue,
Stay right where you are! I'll do you no harm –
I simply desire to pat you.

Just puncture my veins and swallow your fill
For, nobody's going to swot you.
Now, lovely mosquito, stay perfectly still –
A SWIPE! and a SPLAT! and I GOT YOU!

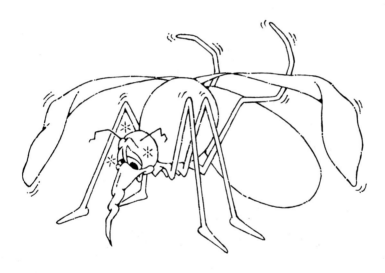

Victor R.I.P.

Remember the fate of Victor McGage
Who ventured too close to the reptile cage.
A hungry old snake took a liking to Victor
So, now he's a lump in a boa-constrictor.

Ethel Earl

A little girl
called Ethel Earl
would ride the escalator,
and there she'd play
till, one sad day,
the escalator ate 'er.

She disappeared,
felt rather weird,
and tumbled out much later
all trembling
resembling
a crinkle-cut potater.

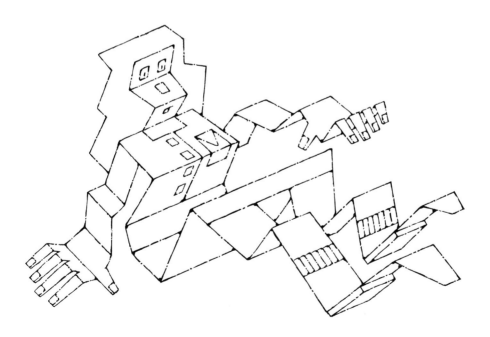

A *Swamp Romp*

Clomp Thump
Swamp Lump
Plodding in the Ooze,
Belly Shiver
Jelly Quiver
Squelching in my shoes.

Clomp Thump
Romp Jump
Mulching all the Mud,
Boot Trudge
Foot Sludge
Thud! Thud! Thud!

Vampire Visit

A pint of blood is all I need
To get me through the night,
A tiny peck around the neck
Will fill me with delight.

I'm sure you have a pint to spare,
Your veins look fairly ample,
So, save a vampire from despair
And let me have a sample.

Please put away that wooden stake,
It looks a trifle sharp.
Be careful now, for heaven's sake,
You'll stab me through the hea-a-a-a-a-a-a-rt!

Shark

Of all the creatures from the Ark
That dwell beneath the sea,
The saddest is the common shark,
Or so it seems to me.

Because he eats voraciously
When swimmers venture near,
He's hunted down ungraciously
With harpoon-gun or spear.

But when we swallow fish and chips
It's valuable to mark –
Beside your chips, cut up in strips
There often sits a shark.

Remember this when next you swim
For, what I say is true –
There's less of you inside of him
Than there is him in you!

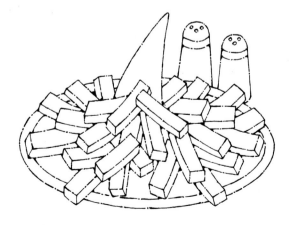

O's

A little b●y called R●bert R●se,
Whenever reading verse ●r pr●se
W●uld ●ften c●l●ur in the O's.
He used a pencil f●r the j●b
And made each O an ●di●us bl●b.

Unhappily f●r R●bert R●se,
He caught a strange disease
Where O's appeared between his t●es
And then behind his knees.

His elb●w, thr●at and then his n●se
Were sl●wly ●vergr●wn with O's,
Then suddenly, ●h w●e, alack!
Th●se ●vals went c●mpletely black.

He died ●f c●urse, which ●nly sh●ws
Y●u sh●uldn't mess ar●und with O's!

Ode to an Extinct Dinosaur

Iguanadon, I loved you,
With all your spiky scales,
Your massive jaws,
Impressive claws
And teeth like horseshoe nails.

Iguanadon, I loved you.
It moved me close to tears
When first I read
That you've been dead
For ninety million years.

Badfairy

A little fairy called last night
When no one was about,
She set my Christmas tree alight
And didn't put it out.

Now, had it been just any tree
I wouldn't really care,
But it was made of P.V.C.
And melted everywhere.

Zookeeper Zack

Zookeeper Zack, I'll give you the sack!
You ought to be fed to the snakes!
You'd make a fine dish for the man-eating fish
And the lions would tear you to steaks.

Your conduct should clearly be treated severely
For, yours is a crime worse than theft.
My beautiful zoo is a wreck, thanks to you
I've hardly an animal left.

In the space of a day, you have chanced to mislay
A zebra, a bear and its mate,
A moose, a piranha, an infant iguana
And something the tiger just ate.

Zookeeper Zack, I'll give you the sack!
But somehow, I think I'd prefer
To throw you inside where the tigers are tied
And wait for the sound of their purr.

Anaconda

A snake to fear
Is the anaconda,
He stretches from here

to over yonder.

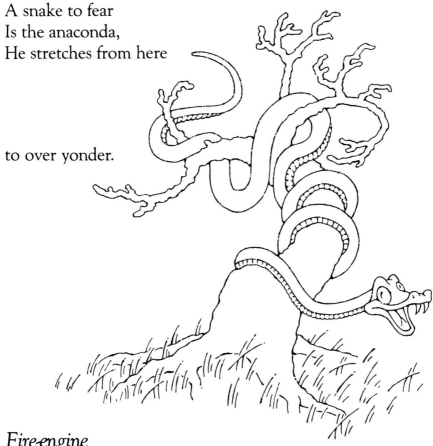

Fire-engine

'Come and see the flashing light
On the fire-engine bright!
See it racing down the road
Carrying its heavy load!'

So said Thomasina Brown,
Just before it ran her down.

Steam-roller Sam

Oh, lend me an ear and I'll happily tell
The story of Steam-roller Sam,
Who handled a steam-roller terribly well
And squashed all his neighbours to jam.

He flattened the Mayor, who was caught unaware,
And flattened the Minister too.
Then, just for good measure, with merciless pleasure,
He ironed the council to glue.

When that was complete, he climbed from his seat
And cackled with murderous zeal.
He danced and he skipped, till he carelessly slipped
And landed in front of the wheel!

The mighty machine gave a murderous scream
And slowly advanced on its victim,
While Sam called aloud to the gathering crowd
Who watched while the Steam-roller fixed him.

So, there is the story of Steam-roller Sam
Whose life had a terrible end,
And where he was flattened, the people sell jam,
A brand which I don't recommend.

The Undertaker

Upon a windy Wednesday night
The undertaker died.
He built a box by candlelight
And locked himself inside.

And as he rode off in the hearse
He contemplated deeply,
'Though dying is a rotten curse,
At least I've done it cheaply!'